Big Brown Bear's
Birthday Surprise

David McPhail

Big Brown Bear's Birthday Surprise

Green Light Readers
HOUGHTON MIFFLIN HARCOURT
Boston New York

The illustrations in this book are done in pen and ink and watercolor.
The display and text type are set in Old Claude.

The Library of Congress has cataloged the hardcover
edition as follows:
McPhail, David, 1940–
Big Brown Bear's birthday surprise/David McPhail.
p. cm.
Summary: An excited Bear mistakenly believes
that Rat has given him a boat for his birthday.
[1. Birthdays—Fiction. 2. Friendship—Fiction. 3. Bears—Fiction.
4. Rats—Fiction.] I. Title.
PZ7.M2427Bg 2007
[E]—dc22   2006004451

ISBN: 978-1-328-89578-3 GLR paperback
ISBN: 978-1-328-89579-0 GLR paper over board

Manufactured in China
SCP 10 9 8 7 6 5 4 3 2 1
4500708306

For Kofi and his uncles, Pepe and Kiko, with love

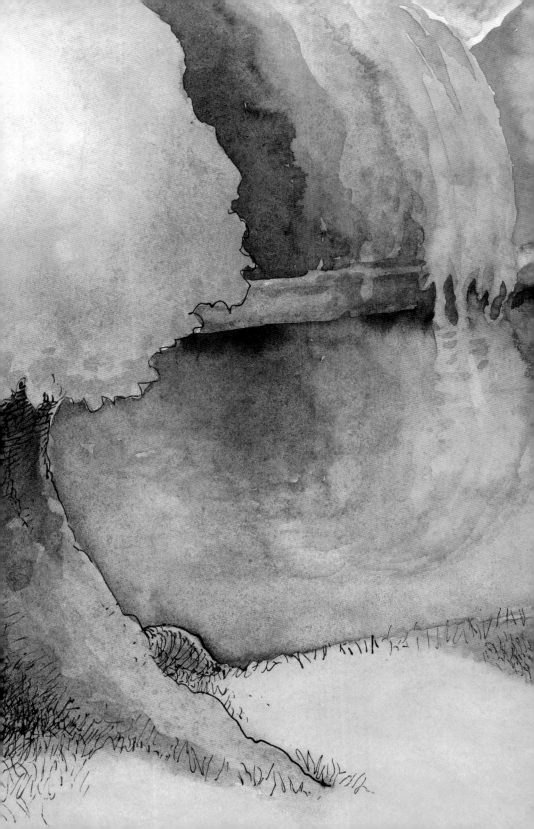

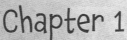

It was a fine summer day. Big Brown Bear and his friend Rat were having a picnic.

"What a good idea this was, Rat," said Bear. "I do so love a picnic."

"Would you like another cucumber sandwich?" asked Rat. "There is one left."

"I suppose I could eat one more,"
Bear replied. "They are my favorite."

"Yes, I know," said Rat.
"That is why I made ten of them."

"What a special day," said Big Brown Bear.
"Indeed," said Rat. "And do you know why it's so special?"
"Why?" asked Bear.

"Because today is someone's birthday," explained Rat.
"Someone I know?" asked Bear.
"Yes," answered Rat. "Someone you know very well."
"Oh, Rat," cried Big Brown Bear, "it's your birthday!"
"Not mine, Bear," said Rat. "It's yours!"

"Really?" asked Bear. "How do you know?"

"I remembered from last year," said Rat. "Birthdays don't change. They are always on the same day."

"Amazing," said Bear.

Chapter 2

Big Brown Bear finished his sandwich,
then lay back on the grass
and closed his eyes.

"Don't go to sleep," said Rat.
"I have a surprise for you."

"What is it?" asked Bear.

"I'll give you a clue," said Rat as he
disappeared into the picnic basket.

"It has four letters and begins with a *B*."

Just then, Big Brown Bear felt
something bump the bottom of his foot.
He sat up and looked. It was a boat!
"Oh, thank you, Rat!" he cried.
"I have always wanted a boat!"

"I didn't get you a boat, Bear,"
said Rat, emerging from the basket.
        But when he looked, Bear wasn't there.
He was sitting in the boat, adjusting the oars.
        "Jump aboard, Rat," Bear called.
"Let's go for a ride!"

Rat saw that the boat was moving away from shore, so he quickly leaped into the seat next to Bear. "As I was saying, Bear," he tried to explain, "this is *not* your boat."

"Whose is it, then?" Bear asked.

"I don't know," said Rat. "It must've gotten loose and drifted downstream."

"Then we'll return it,"
said Bear. "And have
a boat ride, too."

Chapter 3

With Bear working one oar
and Rat working the other, the
boat moved steadily up the river.
"Boating is so much fun,"
said Big Brown Bear.

Just then a hat came floating by.
Bear scooped it up and put it on his head.

Next came a fishing pole. Bear grabbed it
and handed his oar to Rat.
"Row on, will you, Rat?" he asked.
"I would like to fish."

No sooner had Bear dipped his line
into the water than a log drifted into view.
And sitting on the log was a man.

"Hullo!" called Bear. "What a fine day
to be on the river."

"Without a boat it isn't," the man called back. "Hey . . . that's my hat you're wearing!"

"If you say so," said Bear. And he tossed the hat to the man.

"That's my fishing pole, too," the man shouted.

"You're welcome to it," said Big Brown Bear. He held it out for the man.

"And that's my boat!" the man yelled.
"We found it downstream," explained Rat,
"and we were trying to return it."

Rat steered over to the log, and Bear helped
the man climb into the boat.

"I'm glad you came along when you did,"
the man told them. "That log was getting tippy."

With the addition of the man, there was hardly any room to row. Even worse, water was pouring in over the sides.

Rat rowed faster. The man began to bail. But the extra weight was too much, and the boat slowly sank.

Once they'd all swum safely to shore, the man decided he'd had enough boating for one day. He was going home.

"Thanks for rescuing me!" he called over his shoulder.
"Anytime!" Bear called back. "Thank *you* for the boat ride."

Chapter 4

When the man was out of sight,
Bear and Rat headed back to collect the picnic
basket. As they walked along, Bear remembered
something.

"Say, Rat," he said, "this has been a terrific birthday.
But if the boat wasn't my present . . . what is?"

"I'm afraid it's not much of a present," said Rat. "Not compared to a boat."

"Oh, boats are all right," said Bear. "But they can sink."

"You're right about that, Bear," said Rat as he reached into the picnic basket.

"Here is your present," he said, and he handed a ball to Bear.
"Oh, Rat!" cried Bear. "What a beautiful ball!"
"Do you really like it?" asked Rat.
"I do indeed," said Bear.
"Watch this!"

He tossed the ball high into the air,
caught it on the tip of his nose,
and balanced it there
all the way home . . .

. . . where Rat had another surprise waiting.

A Note to Parents & Caregivers—

Reading Stars books are designed to build confidence in the earliest of readers. Relying on word repetition and visual cues, each book features less than 50 words.

You can help your child develop a lifetime love of reading right from the very start. Here are some ways to help your beginning reader get going:

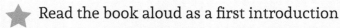 Read the book aloud as a first introduction

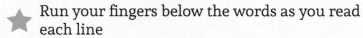 Run your fingers below the words as you read each line

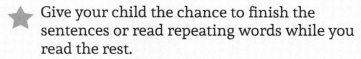 Give your child the chance to finish the sentences or read repeating words while you read the rest.

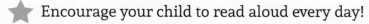 Encourage your child to read aloud every day!

Every Child can be a Reading Star!

Published in the United States by Xist Publishing
www.xistpublishing.com
PO Box 61593 Irvine, CA 92602

First Edition
ISBN: 978-1-5324-0937-0
eISBN: 978-1-5324-0936-3

Monsters Move

Juliana O'Neill
Adam Pryce

xist Publishing

Monsters
move.

5

Monsters

groove.

7

Monsters

mix.

9

Monsters
do tricks.

Monsters
make noise.

13

Monsters
make
toys.

14

15

16

Monsters love art.

18

Monsters love
to fart.

Monsters laugh.

Monsters
take a bath.

Monsters leap.

Monsters sleep.

27

I am a Reading Star
because I can read the
words in this book:

a	mix
art	monsters
bath	move
do	noise
fart	sleep
groove	take
laugh	to
leap	toys
love	tricks
make	

CPSIA information can be obtained
at www.ICGtesting.com
Printed in the USA
LVHW070306250519
618889LV00036B/1252/P